CHILDREN'S DEPARTMENT

j

Bond, Leona
   As tall as a spear

One year on the grasslands of the African Sudan, when the dry land yielded only thorns, Jany's father and the other warriors of the Nuer tribe set off to raid the villages of their "lowly" neighbors, the Dinkas, to steal their cattle for food. "It is easier to eat the meat of cattle that do not belong to us," explained Jany's mother.

When his father not only returned with cattle but with a Dinka boy and girl, Jany was delighted, for he knew that now the boy, Pan, would do most of his household tasks.

Time passes and the successive challenges of daily living bring the two boys together, gradually cementing their friendship. Now that Pan has become like a brother to him, Jany wonders how he could ever have felt such contempt for the Dinkas.

As Jany nears the age of a warrior, he wonders more and more about the true meaning of manhood. How will he be able to raid the neighboring villages, knowing that he might have to capture or even kill a Dinka boy like Pan?

AS TALL AS
A SPEAR

WRITTEN AND ILLUSTRATED BY

LEONA BOND

YOUNG SCOTT BOOKS

Published by Young Scott Books, a Division of
Addison-Wesley Publishing Co., Inc., Reading, Mass. 01867.

Library of Congress Catalog Card No.: 79-141664.
SBN: 201-09120-8.

To My Daughter
Alissa

Contents

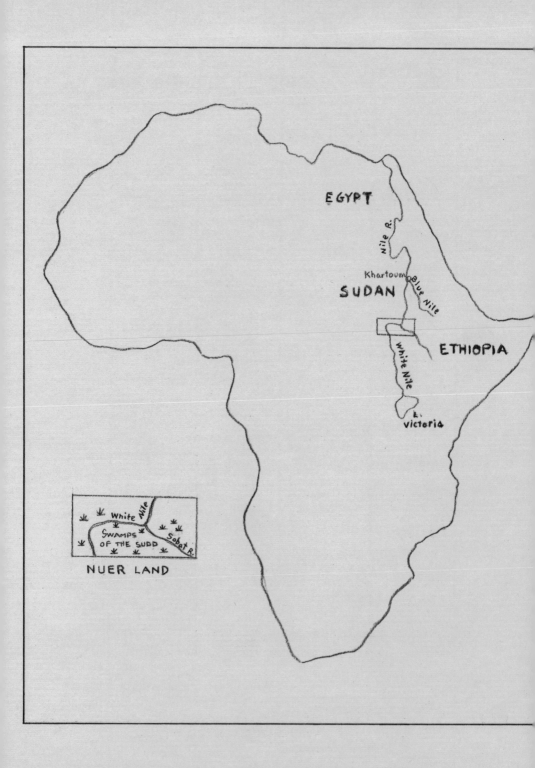

EGYPT

Nile R.

Khartoum
Blue Nile

SUDAN

White Nile

ETHIOPIA

L. Victoria

White Nile

Swamps
of the Sudd

Sobat R.

NUER LAND

Prologue

There is a Nile River in Africa. But before there is a Nile there is a White Nile and a Blue Nile. The Blue Nile starts with many streams washing down the sides of mountains in Abyssinia. The White Nile begins on the equator where the great Lake Victoria feeds it. The White Nile and the Blue Nile come together at the town of Khartoum, in the Sudan, and northward from there to the Mediterranean the river is known simply as the Nile.

The Nuer people live in the grasslands between the Blue Nile and the White Nile. For part of the year it is impossible to reach them, for steamers cannot get through the grass-choked rivers nor can camels walk on the muddy ground. Men find themselves up to their knees in water if they try to cross the grass. So it is little wonder that the people who live in these grasslands are not well known to man. The swamps and grass have offered protection to the Nuer from the raids and conquests of the sultans and pashas and kings who have fought their wars in these lands. The Dinka, another grassland people who hoped to find refuge in the swamps, were not welcomed by the Nuer, who looked upon them as their enemies, for the Dinka came into a land that the Nuer felt belonged to them. The Dinka sought refuge from war only to find new wars and new enemies.

The people of the grass are becoming better known now, for ways have been found to reach them during the past fifty years. While this was happening, Jany was growing up in a land that new ways had not yet reached. This is his story.

1

On the River

As night began to turn into morning of another hot dry day, a mist smelling of wild hyacinth rose from a river crowded with birds still asleep. This river, called the Sobat, is one of many born of drops of rain that form the great River Nile. On the map, it is one of the fingers (or what look like the fingers) of an outstretched hand reaching out over the flat lands and gathering all the waters unto itself.

Here at the headwaters of the Nile there is little water in the rivers when our story begins. It has not rained for a long time—for months—and the only green that shows in the first faint light of the dawn is the slime on the surface of the river. The withered grass will soon be yellow when the sun lights it, the fields straw-colored, the bushes dry as dust, the trees without leaves. It is the winter of the equator.

The hush of the night is still on the land. Though hundreds—it looks like thousands—of dark shapes huddle on the pink surface of the water, all is quiet except for a swishing sound as a bundle of dry twigs moves among them. It bumps against the leg of a heron asleep on one leg, knee-deep in the water. As it stirs it brings a rustle of protest from the sleeping birds around it—a flurry of feathers. A pelican spreads his huge wings, a crane points its beak to the sky. Then silence spreads again.

The bush has moved again though there is no breeze. The sun, moving a little higher into the sky, suddenly strikes sparks of gold from the feathers of the sunbirds in the papyrus along the banks. The birds crowd the river, there is almost no space for the little bush to move

at all. As it cautiously makes its way around a bright blue crane, it catches the wing of a black and white goose in its branches, an Egyptian goose, called the noisiest bird of all by those who know. Rudely awakened, it throws its great wings upward and caws a shattering protest that breaks the peace for all the birds.

The noise, mounting into the morning air, growing louder as storks and hornbills, cranes and ibis, giant fish eagles and white egrets join their protest, becomes deafening.

As the screeching, squawking, hooting, and beating of wings fill the air, the little bush shoots out of the water. It can be seen now that it is tied to the head of a boy. After scrambling for safety up the river bank, he runs as if pursued, and in fact he is, by angry birds not done with complaining. His long legs carry him across the fields, water birds circling over him while bustards and vultures sail far above, too powerful to fear a boy, too mighty to join the uproar below.

The running boy has important news to tell and can not stop to be frightened. He has seen a hammerhead stork! This was the sight he had hoped to see and for which he had disguised and had kept his long cold vigil in the river.

If you saw a hammerhead, it meant that the rains would soon be coming to make the land green again. So at least did his people, who waited each year for the life-giving blessings of rain, believe. And today Jany, for that is the boy's name, had seen the small brown bird. Though it was hard to see among its gaudy fellows, it was more beautiful than all the other birds to those who believed the legend.

The great red ball of the African sun rose higher. Morning had come. The river mists vanished and in the clear light that now touched the birds, their color burst forth as sudden and startling as the noise before.

The birds, wearying of the chase, abandoned him as Jany approached the grass huts of their summer camp strung out along the bank of the Sobat.

He was breathless when he reached the camp, and he threw himself down on the ground in the clearing in front of the hut in which he lived.

His mother dropped the spoon into the pot of porridge she was stirring and, turning to him, asked, "Where have you been?" She saw the bush that covered Jany's head and the leaves and bits of weed that still clung to his damp body.

He laughed at her alarm as he struggled for breath. Then he told her how he had gone among the birds to find the one who foretold the end of the dry season. Her look of alarm changed into delight at the daring and wit of her son. She threw her head back and laughed.

Twittering durra birds fussed around the camp, looking for grain. They perched on the backs of the cows who were waiting for Jany to milk them. They walked among the legs of the sheep and goats that were waiting for food and water.

Jany's father strode out of the hut. "Jany! Where have you been? There is much to be done. What are you doing there on the ground?"

"Come here and listen," Jany's mother called her husband. As he came near, she told him how Jany had spied on the hammerhead, but he did not laugh nor did the story take the frown from his face.

There was too much worry within him to be able to join them in their laughter. There was almost no durra, the grain they ate as porridge at every meal, left in the baskets. Each day he had to take the cattle farther through the dry fields to find grass that was not too coarse for them to eat. The river was so low in places there was hardly enough to water the animals. The greenish muck made it difficult to find water for themselves to drink.

It had been dry before. Every year there came a time when there were only thorns and dust for those who lived on the grasslands.

But this year it seemed that it was a longer and drier time than they had known for many years, though to

people who were always a little hungry, it might seem
so anyway. Jany knew the dry time was too long from
the worry on his father's face.

The little brown stork with its bright promise was not

enough for this man. He wanted to see a cloud in the hot, white sky or the thick dust on the dry ground lifted in swirls by rushing winds. He wanted to look at the sad eyes of his thin cows and feel that he had something more to give them than coarse grass.

He would eat grass himself before he would kill any of his cattle. But there was his family—he could not let them go hungry. He looked at them and saw Jany's eagerness fading from his face, his wife no longer laughing. His eyes sought the dusty ground at his feet. He would have gladly felt the dust in his eyes, his mouth, its pricks and stings on his bare skin, if it were borne by winds promising rain. A warm summer rain would mean the green of new grass, the fragrance of flowers and wild honey, and the palms heavy with fruit again.

His feet stirred the ashes from the cooking fires of many months that covered the ground behind their windscreen. He sighed wearily and left for the kraal.

Jany's mother gave her son porridge in a bowl that had been made of a gourd cut in two and handed him a mussel shell that served as a spoon. As he ate he looked at the peaceful scene all around him. Goats and sheep clustered near the huts, children playing at their feet. Patient cows nuzzled their calves as they nursed them. Women built fires in other clearings. You had to be a Nuer to know that danger lived here too—the danger of hunger. Jany picked up the milking gourds and started toward the cows.

He had almost finished his morning's work when he saw his father at the river's edge, waving him to come. Jany put his gourds in the hut, then ran to join his father, who was pushing their boat into the river.

It had been hollowed out of the trunk of a doum palm and was hardly wide enough to sit in. As Jany steered the light bobbing boat through the water, his father stood in front, a long harpoon raised in his right arm, ready to hurl it at the first glint of a perch that swam in the Sobat. Jany steered carefully between floating clumps of plants and mounds of sand that were just below the surface, while his father kept his eye on the dark green water in which the fish were hiding.

The river was so low that in many places it had turned to marsh with only narrow channels for the little boat. Fish perished as the level of the water sank. Streams that had brought new fish pouring into the river had long since dried up. Once, Jany could have thrown his short fishing spear anywhere at all and it would have found a fish. His mother's basket, dipped into the water at random, would have come out filled with leaping fish spattering drops all over her. Now there were fish only where sudd had piled up into dams and made pools.

Sometimes, Jany knew, for he had done it often, one

could dig in the mud and find fish still alive and good to eat, wriggling in the wet ground. If you tapped on the ground with a little stick the fish would struggle up to the surface thinking it was rain beating on the earth, and if you were quick you could catch one.

Jany's father let fly his harpoon. It caught the flesh of a great perch. Once again his harpoon flashed into the water. And again. He never missed. Jany was proud of his father's skill. He did not have a harpoon of his own, but sometimes he ran out on the grasslands with a long stick broken off an acacia tree. When he threw it he never missed either, for imaginary fish, no matter how large, are not too hard to catch.

As they walked back to camp together, Jany carrying the basket of fish and his father holding his harpoon across his shoulder, Jany asked his father where he was going with the cattle that day.

"Today all the men of the camp go together. Maybe we will try the other side of the river. It is not so deep that they cannot cross." Jany knew this meant that it was no longer safe for anyone to go singly or even in pairs with the cattle. They had to go long distances and into fields they did not know. Lions lay hidden in the grass. Nobody, not even a Nuer, known as the bravest of all the peoples of the grassland, wanted to come upon these beasts by himself.

Jany's father paused under the shade of a tree and ran his hand up the blackened bark of the trunk. Even these trees—the thorn trees—that stayed green when all else had lost their color and were withered with the heat, were losing their leaves. Their crooked gray branches, like skeletal hands, stretched out in all directions for new life from the rainless skies.

Jany's mother came to meet them and as she took the basket of fish from Jany, she too looked at the gray branches and then at her husband.

"It will rain when God wants it to," she told him gently, as if chiding him for his concern.

"We must do something," he said to her. Other men were already leading their cattle out of the kraal and Jany's father ran to meet them, preparing to leave with them.

"What is there to be done?" Jany asked his mother.

She did not answer. She looked out over the plains that she loved—this land of dry grass. This barren, arid land was to her, as it was to most of those who lived on it, the most beautiful and the best land of all. Nuer legend calls it "the barren place of Kwong."

To the east lay the crags of the Abyssinian highlands, dangerous not only because of their deep gullies and rugged cliffs, but because of the white-robed robbers who attacked whatever passed in the valleys below.

To the north lay plains covered with rock where nothing lived except camel drivers seeking loot and slaves. To the south were the stifling jungles filled with the terror of sicknesses they did not know how to cure. One was brought by the tsetse fly that infested the jungles but could not live in the drier grasslands, and so they were safe from it here. From the jungle there sometimes came a sickness that killed their cattle. One year it had almost taken them all, and they could do nothing but watch them die.

This dry land of theirs was after all, the best. She had faith in it. Rain had always come—it would again. She knew that the men would not be content as she was to wait for it. They would go after food, raiding the herds of the Dinka, another tribe, but also cattle people like themselves. It was easier to kill cattle that were not their own.

At last, her eyes still on the distant horizon, she answered her son's question. "What will they do? They will have to go on a raid. They will not wait many days more." To herself she added, "And when they go, may God keep them safe."

2

The Elephant

Jany decided to call for help. He did this reluctantly, for those who would come would laugh at him—and yet how else could he get out of this deep hole? It had not been difficult to climb down, for the men who had dug far down into the earth for their well had left well-marked toeholds. Leaning over the edge, Jany had seen the little steps and had cautiously felt for one with his toe, wondering if it would hold him. Before he realized it he was at the bottom. When he tried to climb back up, however, the toeholds of the men were so far above one another that he could not use them as steps. So there he stood almost twenty feet below the surface of the ground, hating to make a sound. A little girl's face showed at the rim of the hole.

"Is that you, Jany?"

He struck the hard clay with his fist, too angry to answer. In no time at all, his father was there, climbing down to where Jany could reach his outstretched hand.

No word of reproach was spoken, even though the thirsty goats that Jany had left waiting were bleating.

Jany's father spoke to another man. "It is dry as dust at the bottom. It will take more than another day's digging to reach water."

Jany, glad that they paid no attention to him, shooed his little herd toward the river. He was not sure, but it seemed to him that one of those floating logs might be a crocodile. He went farther along the river to where trees grew at the river's edge. As the little goats ran through the high grass, flocks of birds flew up from the grass where they had been invisible during the hot part of the day.

Jany watched them return to the grass where they had been eating the seed. He felt, as they all did here in the grassland, that birds who flew so near to God and must know him best, should not be harmed. He did not know some people hunted birds and killed them and even ate them. It would have shocked him. The Nuer did not eat birds even in the "hungry time."

When they reached the shade, Jany climbed the ryal—the "sausage tree," white people called it—and sat in the deep, leafy shade while the goats daintily stepped into the water. He looked out over the grass and could make out the tops of huts at the camp, just showing over the waving grass. In the distance, someone was leading sheep to the water. Jany climbed higher in his tree and waved wildly. The boy saw him wave and started with his little flock toward him. Jany was glad, for he was tired of being alone.

He was high above the ground and could see beyond the clump of trees at his back. Many times he had sat in the branches of just such a tree, pretending to be a hunter watching for prey, and hurling broken branches down upon the backs of what should have been elephants but were only clumps of loosened tumbleweed. He leaned forward now, stick in hand, ready to hurl it at an enemy behind the trees.

Then he froze in terror. From between the low trees at the edge of the water appeared the long tentative trunk of an elephant and then the huge, wrinkled gray body of the animal itself.

It was not too close yet. If he acted quickly . . . Jany scrambled down from the tree and was racing through the grass before he remembered the goats. They might get trampled, but he could not stop.

"Elephant!" he shouted to the approaching boy, who was startled to see his friend on the ground so far from the tall tree where he thought him to be. "Turn around— go back!" he shouted over his shoulder at the bewildered boy as he kept on running toward the camp. If the wind changed, if the elephant saw either of them and charged,

26

if it saw the camp, it could trample everything—huts, kraals, even the calves. Jany had seen a frightened elephant reduce a village to ruins and trample fields that represented their whole year's grain in an incredibly short time.

"Elephant!" he yelled, again and again, his voice cracking, his chest heaving with hardly enough air to keep him running. But he was heard.

By the time he reached the clearing, a man of his camp ran past him, his spear held high. Others followed. The tall grass, silent under the noonday sun a short while ago, was suddenly alive with shouts and the sounds of running feet, with women calling to their children, excited animals baa-ing and bleating, dogs barking everywhere. Jany, in spite of the blood pounding in his ears, turned around and ran back after the men. His mother saw him but did not call him back. She knew that he would not listen.

The men were far ahead, their long legs easily outdistancing him. When they had almost reached the elephant, they spread out into a semicircle. Still running, they fell into perfect formation without needing to shout an order or exchange a word. This they had done many times before.

Jany's father had left that morning with the cattle for the other side of the river and by now was far away. Were he there, Jany felt sure, he would be the first to run upon the elephant, his spear would be the first strike, his the first voice raised to warn the beast of his fate.

The semicircle grew smaller as the men, with spears raised, drew together and closed in on the animal. Trapped by the river at its back, the desperate elephant trumpeted a fearsome complaint against its fate.

The men drew closer still, shutting off any chance of escape. As Jany watched, a spear flew across the small space between the men and the elephant. If it charged, it could kill any one of them. But the spear hit. A dozen more were thrown—all found their mark. The huge beast crashed to the ground with spears sticking out of it on all sides. The man who had hurled the first spear would be hailed as its killer, though no one could say which deadly point had found the heart of the animal now dying on the river bank, its blood mingling with the slime and ooze of the river where it had come to find a cool drink.

The young boys, who had not been initiated into manhood and had not been given their spears, stared at the men who had killed the elephant. How fine they had looked, heads thrown back, unafraid, in full view of an animal that could have trampled any one of them to death in a few seconds! Jany's eyes shone in admiration for them all—his people!

The men skinned the animal and began to cut it up

so it could be divided among those who were there. The one who was honored as the killer would get the tusks— but meat belonged to everyone.

So Jany had a part to take home. He gathered together the flock of goats almost forgotten at the water's edge and started home.

He was bringing meat to his mother and he was glad. But what if it were a victor's spoils? He longed to be part of the world he could only guess at—the world his father entered when he took his spear in hand—a world of half-shadows that Jany could imagine only dimly.

Sometimes his father would rise before dawn to join others and disappear into the dark shadows that covered the land at that early hour. A few days later he would return with strange oxen. Jany could only guess where he had been.

He remembered a night not long ago when a friend came to their door and in hoarse, strangled tones called to his father, who had then taken his spear and had followed him into the night. That time he brought back no cattle, but he had said in answer to Jany's questions that his friend's honor was saved.

That was important, Jany knew, though he did not know how honor could be won—or lost. He knew because he had heard it said many times that the Dinka had no honor. They were cowards and hunted at night, sneaking up on their victims when they could not be seen. He had heard that they used traps to catch animals—what Nuer would?—and that they spread snares when they feared raids on their cattle. This was shameful.

Cowards! Jany's chest swelled with pride at his own courage. No cowardly Dinka he! Yet he remembered what he had heard an old man say, and the doubt it had started in his mind. He could almost hear the old man's voice now in back of his memory and could see again his kindly face lit by dancing firelight:

"Oh, yes, the Dinka they are cowards—for they do not like danger. And they stay far away from it if they can. They do not go to meet danger as we do." Then he added, "And they do not get killed as often as we do, either. Cowards? Well, maybe they are. Or maybe they are smarter than we are. This is hard to know."

3

The Raid

The fire behind their windscreen had gone out, but it did not matter for there would not be many mosquitoes until the first rains came.

It had been a happy evening, a night of feasting and song and dancing. Jany had joined in the "Cow Dance," his arms raised to look like the long horns of their cattle. As he danced he had pretended that he was a beautiful white ox as strong and brave as the eagle they called "Ku-Ee" that flew over their river. Jany would name his ox after it. When he had an ox.

Jany lay on his goatskin beside his father, who slept the sleep of utter exhaustion, flat on his back, his arms flung wide. Today he had walked many miles in the hot, unshaded grasslands looking for good grass for the cattle to eat.

Jany could not sleep. It may have been the restlessness of the cattle tethered nearby. They did not sleep either. Perhaps the new moon would rise in the sky the next

evening. Jany knew, as all his people did, that the oxen and cows could see the moon a full day before it showed itself to men, and it was said that this made them restless.

Jany was restless too. That evening at the milking, Jany had seen his father walk among his oxen, patting their sides, fondling the curved horns. He stopped before a black one for a long time.

He was saying good-bye to him, Jany thought. He will kill him tomorrow as a sacrifice, and this meant only one thing—a raid for the cattle of a Dinka village some place far away. The ox offered so generously must ensure their success. Jany fell asleep at last and dreamed of riding a black ox in the sky toward a gleaming star that they never reached.

The next day was a very hot one, and Jany, who had slept little during the night, found it hard to do his work, to be patient with the animals who were hot and fretful themselves.

As the day wore on, Jany fished and even joked with the boys on the dam as they threw their spears at the fish below, but his mind was elsewhere. A day would come and it could not be far off—perhaps after the rains came and went once more—and he would be given his spear. Then his father would say to him on the night before a raid, "Come when I call you at dawn." He would be ready!

34

Even this day started to draw to a close. Jany drove the goats and sheep into the kraal, then went for the milking gourds. He saw no spear hanging on the wall next to the gourds! Suddenly the blood was pounding in his head, his heart beating fast.

"Mother!" She turned to see him pointing to the wall as he ran toward her. She understood.

"No, no," she said. "He has not gone yet. Go and tell him the fire is in the pit and all is ready for the ox." She did not share Jany's excitement; her voice was low, her face unsmiling. She did not go with Jany to watch the sacrifice.

Jany found his father in the grass beyond the row of huts. He sat sharpening his spear on a rock surrounded by friends—those who had been initiated with him and who would form an informal raiding party.

Jany's father called to him, and Jany settled down near him to hear the talk of the men about war and their tales of adventure. He loved to listen—it was as if he were being told his own future.

"Jany, do you know where hunger came from?" Rol, a friend who had known Jany since his birth, leaned toward him and tapped his knee. "Listen and I will tell you. Once, a long time ago, Man had no stomach and so he was never hungry. Man's stomach lived apart. It lived in the bush and it ate very little—a few small insects,

35

sometimes a date or a fig. Even when it found honey, it just tasted it.

"Man watched Stomach and pitied it because it had so little to eat. Oh, that was a bad mistake! When Man took Stomach home with him and gave him food, it wanted more—and more. Stomach became part of Man after that, and Man had to work hard to give it all it wanted. Man has to go out to find food for Stomach all the time now."

They all laughed. Rol added, "You can see Stomach rules us. I am hungry again."

Jany's father took his sharpened spear and led the way to the kraal where the black ox waited.

Rol said to him as he brought the spear close to the animal's throat, "If the heart is sad at what you are about to do, remember that Stomach will be happy."

Jany's father called on the spirits to bless his spear called Kir, which had been in his family for many generations. Then he drove it quickly into the animal's neck. He turned away from the bleeding ox. He had loved it, but he had done what he had to do.

* * * * *

Much later that evening, people sat or lay around the dying fire, talking in low tones, telling stories, occasionally glancing at the clear, cloudless sky that still held no promise of rain.

A young man named Gee stood up and, holding an ox bell high above his head, walked around the group singing praises to his ox. His voice was strong and full of feeling, for he loved his ox though he had not yet seen it. The bell and the song and the name were already picked out—for an animal yet to be captured.

An old man who was fond of speaking of the Dinka prepared to tell a story. Everyone knew which story he was about to tell, and they had heard it before, but it was a story they never tired of hearing.

"At one time—it was a very long time ago," the old man began, "when God could talk to his people and not only to the birds in the heavens, God loved the Dinka as much as he loved the Nuer. They were both his sons and equal in his eyes." He paused and looked around. He had everyone's attention. He continued.

"God, wishing to give presents to the sons he loved, called them to him and promised to give an old cow to the Dinka and its beautiful young calf to the Nuer. The Dinka was not pleased, but he did not show his feelings, and thanked God, as did the Nuer. Then in the dark of the night he stealthily crept to God's cattle byre. Outside it he imitated the voice of the Nuer. You know how crafty a Dinka can be!

37

"So God, thinking it was the Nuer, sent out the young calf to him. When the Nuer came for the calf, God found out how he had been tricked, and his anger was terrible. The Nuer, left with the old cow, was also angry. God spoke to him and said, 'You must avenge yourself on the Dinka for this deception. You will raid the Dinka's cattle and do this until the end of time.'"

Jany did not hear the end of the story. He was asleep.

When he awoke his father was gone with his friends and with Gee, who was seeking his first ox.

4
Waiting

There is a place on the Sobat River where the wild date palms grow. Jany loved the sweet fruit and came often to eat his fill. Today he brought baskets to fill with wild fruit and perhaps a few bush yams to take back to his mother.

This would be their supper tonight, for they had to save what little durra remained.

It was cool where the palms were thickest, and after filling his baskets, Jany lay down to rest. Looking at the patterns the leaves made against the sky he thought of his father and wondered where he was at that moment. He could not think his father might be in danger—he had no doubt that his father was the strongest and bravest of all—but he wondered about the misty land he had so often heard about and never seen. Dinkaland lay to the north of the Sobat, almost to the White Nile.

Arabs sometimes came to the shores of the Sobat when the ground was not too muddy for their camels' hooves, bringing beads and bracelets and iron for new spears. They talked of the desert and of the green banks of the Nile and of new buildings in the city, Khartoum, with white columns and many floors. Khartoum was no longer a place of muddy paths and little white houses, they said, but a place where thousands lived and where many came to learn new things at the schools.

One day a tax collector had come on his steamboat and tried to explain why he needed to take some of their cows. He told Jany and those who listened that there were buildings his English government had built where writing was taught and other buildings where the sick could be healed—and even buildings to hold money, though this they did not understand at all.

As Jany watched the papyrus reeds sway in the air and looked at the garlands of fig trees that grew like vines over the acacias on the shore, the present seemed less real to him than the stories about other places that he had heard.

A herd of giraffe, their heads just visible above the grass, showed in the distance. In no time they were at the river. Jany lay quiet and watched them as they bent their long necks to drink the water. Its smell on a wayward breeze had brought them here. They were safe, even this close to camp, for their hooves left no mark on the hard, dry ground and they could not be tracked.

After the rains started they would not be safe, for they could be hunted and killed. This year Jany knew that he could go with the men of his camp when they tracked giraffe. He was so close to them now that he could see their velvety eyes and hear them drinking. He watched a baby nuzzle its mother and thought that killing giraffe might not give him the joy he had thought it should.

He felt ashamed of his doubts. He asked the empty grass, was anything better than bravery? Nobody heard his question and nobody answered it.

He jumped up, picked up his basket, and started back, keeping himself company with visions of himself hurling spears at enemies and huge beasts. Birds feeding on the seed that lay scattered among the dead grasses rose from the ground as he walked. A little farther along he came upon his mother, filling her water gourds at the river. She had had to come this far for clear water.

She put a full gourd atop her head, then balancing another on her hip, she walked to where Jany waited for her, and they started back.

"How long will father be gone?" Jany knew that his mother did not know, but he had to ask for it was all he could think of.

She answered not his words, but his mood. She understood how he felt. For her too the heat was oppressive. The water was low, the stored grain almost gone, the cattle limp and almost too fretful to be milked. It was a time for worry. Leopards and lions were too close to their camp on the river—the men were too far.

"Tomorrow you will come here and find clay and we will make new pots. We must get ready for the rain, which will come soon."

Rain. As she spoke Jany saw again in his mind's eye their house in the village where they lived. He saw again the large house with the round roof—the byre for the cattle—and the smaller house where he lived. He imagined green corn and millet and streams of fresh water running through the fields of grain. He could almost smell the damp earth.

The next day Jany searched the river banks and found the clay his mother wanted and brought it to her. She rolled it into long ropes between her two palms and then coiled the ropes round and round. She stopped and wet her fingers and shaped and smoothed the ropes of clay. Jany watched the coils become tall jars.

People gathered around. Neighbors sat down to talk, and always it seemed to Jany, they talked of the weather. He was glad to escape with two companions, boys about his age who would no doubt join him in the initiation ceremonies. Cor and Kot and Jany chased one another in an exuberant game of tag, pushing and tripping each other.

Suddenly Cor dropped to the ground and covered his face with his hands in mock fear. "I am afraid," he whimpered, as the others laughed at him, "I am a Dinka—do not take my oxen please!"

Jany pushed him over, and as Cor jumped up, the three boys ran over the fields, shouts of "Thief!" "Dinka!" "Coward!" reaching the camp.

Jany's mother heard—and frowned. "I do not like their game," she said to a little girl who came up to her with a basket of fish. She patted the little girl's head, her frown giving way to a smile.

"Thank you for the fish. You must have some grain to take home with you," she said. "Jany!" she called. "Come here!"

He came reluctantly, took the gourd he was handed and went to their storage baskets. The little girl who followed him exclaimed, "You have so little left!"

"It is enough," Jany said impatiently, but his fingers scraped the bottom as he dipped his hands into the baskets again.

She accepted the grain, for she knew there was none in her hut.

Later when dusk stole over the land, bringing coolness with it, and Jany once again bent to the cows for their milk, the little girl crept up behind him and laid something at his feet. She turned and quickly ran away.

Jany picked it up. It was a bracelet made of giraffe hair. He put it on his arm knowing that he would not really be allowed to wear it until he had joined the ranks of the initiated.

He showed it to his mother as they sat together at their evening meal. "Mother, I cannot keep it," he said.

"You must keep it," she replied. "It would not do to return it. Who is more honored than he who gives? You must let others be generous if they wish. For to have nothing is to be most adorned." She reflected for a moment, then added, "It must belong to Gee, her brother, who went with your father." She laughed gently. "Gee is generous, too."

After their supper they sought coolness along the river bank and walked into the darkening plains. They smelled the lilies in the heavy air and listened to the sound of snakes slithering into the water and the hum of hundreds of insect wings.

It grew darker and they knew that they should turn back, but still they walked on. They knew, as every Nuer knew, that the dark was dangerous. The velvety evening air that seemed so peaceful hid many things— scorpions, snakes, potholes, sharp thorns, fallen branches that lay hidden, and the bright eyes of wakeful lions who had slept during the day and now sought their food. The grasslands seem empty only to a stranger.

45

Still they lingered. Suddenly Jany's mother grabbed his shoulder and, pointing, said, "Look there!"

Jany peered toward the shrouded horizon where she pointed. White mists across a purple sky made everything unclear, yet he was sure he saw something moving in the distance. A dust cloud? Stray cattle? But no one would leave cattle out this late. It must be cattle, Jany thought, as he made out the long curved horns. What cattle would be alone, exposed to the terrors of the grass?

They were not alone! With a happy cry Jany raced across the grass, unmindful of its dangers and his mother's restraining call.

It was his father coming home, and Jany ran to meet him. Jany ran so fast it was but minutes before his father's arms lifted him into the air, as if he were still a little boy, and they exchanged eager questions as he set Jany down again. They started back and were met by women and children running toward them from the camp, for news had traveled fast.

Gee, whose bracelet lay at this moment under Jany's goatskin, walked proudly behind a sleek red ox whose black horns rose majestically above his head. He had captured it on his first raid—he would never have a prouder possesion. It was worthy of the tassels and bell he had made for it.

Success and a safe return—is it any wonder eyes shone and people burst into song, Jany among them?

Yet, not all were happy. Coming up from behind there was a strange boy. He held the hand of a tall, sad-eyed girl who walked beside him. They did not smile, or sing, or even talk.

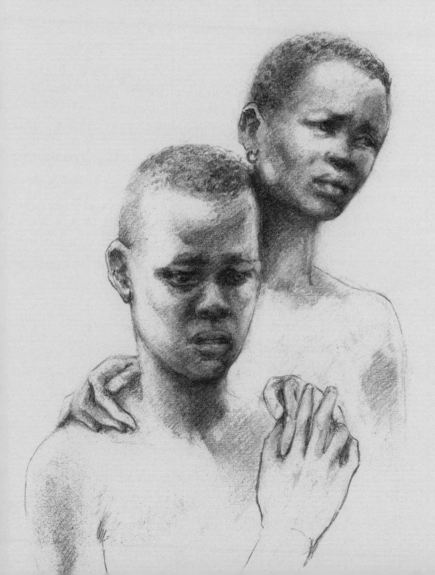

5

The Captives

It was a clear, starry night. The men who had been on the raid sat around the fire and waited for their supper while the others crowded around them, eager to hear them tell of their adventure.

Laughter rose in the air while the birds listened. There was boastful talk and exclamations of admiration and surprise as the story of the raid was told over and over again.

They had taken the Dinka in this village near the White Nile completely by surprise while they slept in the heat of the day. The Dinka had scattered for cover, offering no resistance. Then they had had to hunt the cattle down where they were hidden in the deep grass. Here and there a man ran at them with a spear as he saw his cows being led away.

Jany's father pointed at the new boy and girl. "I have brought them with me. I did not want to leave them behind. They did not run off with the others." He paused, and then said, "We will need extra hands when the rains begin—they will be useful for they will work for us."

"Then they belong to us?" Jany asked. Jany's mother glanced at him quickly. She did not like his haughty tone, and as if to show her displeasure, she filled two bowls with porridge, found spoons, and handed them to Jany.

"Take this food to them," she ordered.

Jany did as he was asked, but when he stood in front of the Dinka captives he would not bend down to hand them their food. The Dinka boy, though he must have been hungry, did not lift his eyes from the ground, nor reach for his porridge. The girl did, looking into Jany's eyes with her own sad ones.

Jany had also displeased his father with his tone and manner. These two were captives. This much was indeed true. But he did not feel, nor want Jany to feel, that they were *owned*. People could not be, should not be, owned, he felt.

"Must they do whatever I tell them?" Jany, not knowing his father's thoughts, asked his question, and Jany's father sought his wife's eyes with a mute appeal for help.

"They will live with us, and they will help us. That is all," she said sharply. She was troubled. There were many among them, some sitting at this moment around their fire, who had been brought from Dinka villages.

Some of them had come of their own accord, forced to leave their homes because of famine. Sometimes they came because of Arabs who burned the houses they lived in. Many tragedies had scattered people and brought them to other lands. She herself had been born to a woman who had been brought to the Nuer just as this girl had been tonight. Had she never told Jany this?

She had not. To tell him would have been difficult, and she had let the time slip by. Now he thought all Dinka were worthless. She stared into the fire and knew that she had not cared before when the people around her showed hatred and scorn. Hatred was a senseless feeling, but it existed everywhere. It was different now that her own son had learned to hate. His scornful laughter had fallen upon her ears and had made her heart heavy with sadness. It mattered very much now.

Jany did not know of his mother's thoughts. As he hung now on his father's words and heard his father tell of his daring, Jany's eyes were bright with admiration. As his father looked into the boy's shining eyes, he felt he had done well after all. He reached into the cooling ashes of fire that had long since died down and rubbed Jany's back with them. This would keep the flies from biting and let him sleep.

At last Jany's mother roused herself and handed Jany a goatskin. "Give this to the new boy—and show him where he can sleep." She beckoned to the girl who rose and followed her into the hut.

There was not much space between the windscreen and the hut, and Jany had to spread the goatskin near his own. The guests had left, the fire had gone out, and Jany's father had fallen asleep. Only he and the new boy were awake, and the new boy did not move or speak or approach the goatskin.

Jany lay down and looked into the darkness of the sky above him. "I will not have to water the goats or clean the kraal," he thought, but joy did not come to his heart. The silent, huddled figure at the end of the little clearing made Jany uncomfortable, but at last he slept.

The next morning Jany discovered that the new boy needed no urging to do his tasks. He seemed eager to be occupied. He cleaned the floor inside the hut and emptied the ashes from the fireplace. He cleaned the kraal after the animals left it and spread new sand over it. He gathered the dung and spread it in the sun so that it would dry for the fires they would light that evening.

He swept the ground free of thorns and termites where the babies played. He carried water for the cows to drink when they were brought in from the fields at dusk. He filled water gourds for Jany's mother at the river. He milked the cows and learned how to churn the butter when his sister was too busy to do it.

When Jany's father went back to digging the well, the boy carried the dirt away in baskets and spread it on the floor of the kraal, stamping it down over the dust.

As the days passed the new boy became part of their lives. He dipped his fingers into the fresh milk and let the littlest children lick it from his fingers. He carried them on his back to their mothers when they were called. He held them on the backs of the fattest goats and let them ride into the grass. When they fell off, he brought them to his sister, whose name was Gia, and she would give them a lick of honey from her cooking pot and soft words from her smiling lips.

He was gentle with the oxen when he picked the flies and ticks from their sides. He brushed them and whispered into their ears until they grew quiet while Gia milked them.

Sometimes when Gia churned the milk into butter, she watched her brother. He never laughed with the children he made happy, and when he soothed the cows his own face was drawn and anxious.

One morning as she carried the newly churned butter to the storage pots, she called her brother. As he helped her add to the curds already stored and still fresh in the earthenware vessels, she said to him: "Try not to care too much. They are good to us—perhaps they will learn to love us." Her eyes were full of kindness as she went on, "They must love you—you are so good." His face did not relax. "You know we have nobody in the world. We were alone, without mother or father, before we were brought here. This may become home for us. There is a mother here—and a father."

Her eyes were full of tears and she looked away, for she was old enough to remember their mother before she had been taken with smallpox. She had never known her father, for he had been carried away by Arabs when they came raiding for slaves.

She looked again at her brother and knew that words alone could not comfort him. Still, she added, "We are still together." He touched her hand, but his face remained sad.

The days passed free of work for Jany who now had nothing to do but to make himself happy. He fashioned little cows and little byres out of clay and he made himself a large herd and thought up heroic names for his cattle, making up songs for them. He hunted for honey, figs, and dates and looked for seeds in the dry grass to string into bracelets.

Sometimes he joined the others fishing on the dam, though more for company than to fish, for there were too few fish to catch anything.

He listened for hours to the stories men told of battles fought and won and of strange people to the north—Arabs in flowing gowns, white men who turned red at many things—the hot sun, insect bites, anger, and with a fever that seized them.

One day he heard that Arabs were in a camp near his and he set off with his clay cattle to see them. The Arab traders were old men, but they talked of their youth

when they rode into battle on camels over deserts strewn with bodies. Jany did not understand all they said, but he listened until it grew dark. He slept that night in this strange camp with other boys his age, boys who would be initiated with him when the time came, for they were Nuer, too. He dreamt of battles, and when he made his way home along the river the next morning he wondered what wars there would be for him to fight in when he grew up.

He gave his mother the beads the Arabs had traded him for his clay toys, but ran away when she showed him the empty water gourds.

The hot days passed in a golden haze punctuated only with games and pleasure, and Jany grew more restless and more irritable.

One evening Jany stood at one end of the kraal and watched the new boy try to milk a restless young cow who would not be still.

"That is not the way!" he said, coming forward, but the new boy did not turn around, for he did not know he had been spoken to. Jany called louder but he still did not turn around. "I don't know his name," Jany realized with some surprise. "I have never asked it."

He came and stood where he could be seen. "Let me show you," he said, and slipped a rope around the back legs of the cow. Then he pulled the rope tight so that the legs came together and she could not move. He handed the rope to the boy, who took it.

"Keep it tight," Jany told him. "What is your name?" he asked as he picked up the milking gourd and squatted down to milk the cow. He asked the question casually, as if it had just occurred to him.

The new boy said in a voice that could hardly be heard, "It is Pan." Feeling that it wasn't friendliness that had made Jany ask and angry at the other's scornful tone during the past days, he added with a fierce pride, "I belong to a great clan named for the eagle of the Nile, Ku-Ee."

Jany stared at him. "That cannot be—that is my clan. And you . . ." His voice trailed off, but his meaning was clear to Pan. How could a captive, dirtied with the dust of the kraal, belong to his clan?

"Here, you do the rest," Jany said to the boy whose feelings he had just hurt, for he wanted to get away from someone he had made unhappy.

He went in search of his father. "Can it be true—can Pan belong to our clan?" he asked him, and his father told him that it could be true.

"It is well known," his father told him, "that the Dinka people had clan names and clan animals long before we thought to."

Then his father gave Jany a drink from the well,

which at last had been finished and had water in it. Jany drank and filled his gourd again and started for the kraal with it. Something made him stop and spill the water on the ground. "Dinka!" he muttered.

Jany's father picked up the gourd and filled it. "Take it to him," he ordered. Jany took the water and looked at his father. He turned and walked to the kraal.

Pan looked at the water as if he would not take it. He looked beyond Jany and saw Jany's father standing behind him. He carried his harpoon and two fishing spears, and he was watching him and smiling.

"You must be hot—take it and drink it, and we will go fishing," Jany's father said, and Pan took the gourd from Jany's hand. Then Jany's father gave him a spear, and as Jany watched, feeling left out of something he wanted to understand, Pan broke into a smile and ran toward the river.

Jany followed his father. It seemed to Jany that he had done what was right, acted as he was expected to behave, and yet it had been wrong, after all.

6

Rain!

Lily pads parted in front of their narrow boat, clinging to its sides. The ibis and herons watched them, unmoving, and ostriches stood on the bank and waved them by with their glorious wings. The finches and the diochs, those the Nuer called durra birds because they ate their seeds, rose in hordes protesting the passage of the little boat. The sweet smell of the yellow hibiscus lay in the quiet air like a happy memory too fragile to be recalled.

It was peaceful on the river. Nothing stirred, not even the feathery tops of the papyrus that bowed to the lightest wind. Monkeys chattered at them from the palms as they drifted past.

Jany felt easier with himself as his pole dipped into the water and he watched his father spear a silvery fish with perfect aim. He glanced once or twice at Pan who sat behind him, looking for fish from the rear of the boat, but he said nothing.

They tied up the boat and started toward the camp. It

was so still, so quiet as the sunshine turned a deeper, metallic gold, it seemed that time itself had ceased.

Suddenly a cool wind made them shiver. In moments the air was filled with screeching birds. Clouds that seemed to appear from nowhere moved rapidly across the sky, casting racing shadows across the grass.

Jany felt it first—on his nose. Then it touched an up-turned palm. Another trembled on an eyelash. Drops of rain!

The dust that had lain so long under the hot sun escaped into the wind and stung their skin before the pelting rain could imprison it on the ground. Drops began to fall regularly now, hard as little stones, wherever they struck.

They turned their faces to the new rain, spread out their arms and stood glistening and wet as the rain ran down their bodies in little streams. This miracle, which occurred every year, filled them each time with a shock of surprise and wonder.

Jany's father looked up at the sky and spoke for them all. "God, rain well! It is your world."

Already little gullies that had been filled with dust now ran with fresh streams of water. This parched, cracked earth would be beautiful tomorrow. It would be a new green world painted with flowers of brilliant pink and yellow and purple—more flowers than anyone could count. The animals would be sleek and shining, and everywhere people, refreshed and happy in the washed air, would sing.

*　*　*　*　*

Each year when the rivers, full of rain, overflowed for miles around and the dry grasslands turned into marshes and swamps, it became time for the Nuer to return to their villages on the "high ground." Although there were no real hills on the flat, endless plains of Nuerland, there were ridges of sand inland, beyond the reach of the floods, that had been formed by the gales that came with the rains every year. Here, on these ridges, the Nuer had built their permanent homes.

Jany's father stood in front of their little hut with Jany beside him and looked at the sky with a practiced eye. "It will still be many days before the real rains," he said, more to himself than to his son. "Too soon to bring the cattle to the village, for the rains have had no time to make drinking streams for them." He rubbed his chin. "Still, the fields will take much work . . ." He came to a decision.

"Jany, you will stay and take care of the herds. I will kill an ox so there will be meat for you here. I will take Pan and he will work with me. Then when all is ready I will send him for you."

62

No one knew when the real rains would come, but they must make ready for them. This was a time of worry for all. After the first joy at the miracle the rains had already wrought came the knowledge that the rain, the wayward rain, might not come again for many weeks. Or when it came, it might fall in such great gushings that it would flood and drown the new plants they would soon be making haste to grow.

There might still be a drought. The new green which now stretched away on all sides could change again into a hard, cracked, empty plain, haunted by hungry animals.

Jany's father was ready to leave. He had his spear—it was knife, axe, tool, and protector to him wherever he went. He placed a roll of skins across Pan's back and, joined by others who were leaving, started the trek on foot to their permanent village. Jany watched them as long as he could. On the open, treeless plain it was a long time before they disappeared from view.

Jany's mother called him, "Come, come—there is much to do. There will be many at our fire tonight. Your father has sacrificed an ox so that it will rain well for us. Who will watch it in the pit? Who will fetch the water from the well—and feed the lamb born today?"

Turning back to her fire, she almost fell over the little girl who was Gee's sister. She took the little girl's hand and said to her, "Come help me water the goats."

The little girl stood her ground. She had something important to say and would not move till she had said it.

"My brother, Gee, came home from the raid with a beautiful ox."

"Yes, yes, I know—and he is very proud of it," Jany's mother said impatiently. "Now come."

The little girl did not take the proffered hand and said quite clearly, looking up at Jany's mother, "He is going to give it to you!"

Jany's mother stared at her. "What are you saying? Don't you know he prizes that ox? A young man with the ox of his first raid—give it away? Nobody gives an ox away." She looked at the sly smile on the little girl's face. Nobody gives an ox away unless . . . The little girl's meaning began to dawn upon her.

The little girl knew that she was understood at last.

"My brother has said that there is a beautiful girl at your fire now," the little girl said, "and it is true."

"You think your brother Gee wants to marry my Gia? And is already thinking of oxen for the bride-price?" Jany's mother said "my Gia" as naturally as if the girl were indeed her daughter. "I think of her so," she realized, a little surprised at herself for not knowing it sooner. "She has made herself one of us," she thought.

The little girl had more to say. "Gee will not come to sit by your fire or eat with you any more."

65

Then it was true. There could be no doubt, for this is the way a young man who is courting must behave. This is the way he is expected to show respect for the man he hopes to be his father-in-law.

"Well, well," Jany's mother said as she turned over the thought of the marriage in her mind. Gia was not their daughter. Could they accept the bride-price when Gee offered his oxen to them? Gia was not their daughter—but she was loved, Jany's mother knew, and they would find a way.

7
The Cattle Return

This was to be the day! Jany felt the sunlight on his eyelids but kept his eyes closed a little longer as he slowly awoke to the thought of what this day was to mean. There was sun at last! The cattle drive could begin. To-day he was going home!

He opened his eyes. Sunshine flooded the earth, sparkled on the river, turned their straw huts to gold, and opened the flowers.

Jany jumped up and shook Pan, sleeping beside him. Pan had returned a few days ago with the news that his father was prepared for their homecoming. Then rain had come, in short angry bursts. Threatening clouds had hung over the grassland and hid the sun until today.

This was the day. The rain had watered the earth and the cattle would find water to drink on their long walk home—and grass. It was still dry enough for them to move over the ground without becoming mired in bogs or puddles, but it would not stay this way for long.

"We must get ready," Jany said in a fever of impatience. "We must start." So many things could happen and all of them were in his mind now.

They had to reach the village before dark. It was a long way and the cattle would not be safe in the grass at night. They must be kept moving and must not be allowed to browse too long or wander off where their fancy took them. They had to be kept together; it would be easy for one or two or three of them to vanish from view where the grass called the devil's horsewhip grew tallest.

At the kraal, Jany looked over the cattle. These placid cows whom he knew so well looked strange today. Would they listen when he called their names? Maddened by flies and mosquitoes that swarmed everywhere from the puddles which spawned them, would they bolt into the grass? Would they be frightened by the snakes that lay coiled in the potholes? Would the great sharp thorns hurt their feet and cripple them? Would the birds that rode on their backs distract them? And what of lions?

Jany's excitement rose. He could not stand it any longer. The women, gathering together their possessions, laughing and gossiping as they put out the fire and took up the skins from the ground, seemed to him like mindless children. When would they start? Were they waiting

68

for the sun to set? The sun was already in the sky—it was already late, very late!

Pan was suddenly at his side. Other young men—some boys—appeared from nowhere. The cattle were massing, someone gave a signal, whistles mingled with the lowing of the cattle and then with the noise of their hooves. The drive had started.

Heart pounding, chin raised, Jany fell into step beside the cattle. He did not look back. Leaving a place where one has lived, even one that had been a home for a little while, is also leaving a part of one's life behind. Jany's excitement was not too great for him to feel a pang of sadness.

Pan ran up and down alongside the herd and, with a long pole, shooed them into formation. He pleaded and coaxed and called them by name and was swifter than the friskiest calves who tried to find their own way into the grass. As Jany watched him he realized that Pan was a wonderful cowboy. He knew very little about him, Jany thought. His bed had been beside his own, he had eaten at the same fire, they had worked side by side, but Jany had not wondered about him and so knew nothing.

Now he was curious as he walked and watched. "Does he miss his home?" he began. He threw away these new thoughts. They revealed a weakness. Pan was a captive —a Dinka captive—a cowardly, sneaking . . . . The worn-out phrases that he had heard and laughed at and even spoken so many times seemed to have no meaning today.

Jany had no more time to think, for Cor ran by after a calf heady with excitement in the new grass. Jany followed, and when Cor headed the calf off, Jany caught it as it tried to barge between his legs. Still holding the calf, Jany fell into step beside Cor.

Jany couldn't think of anything to say. Cor and he had made fun of many things, many people. Cor was a clown who had often delighted Jany with his mimicry. Now Jany remembered how they had made fun of Pan and the memory caused him pain. He remembered the words of scorn, the contorted faces which Pan had not seen.

He raised his long pole and slashed the air with it. It did not help. It is not so easy to cut off painful images. Jany was close to not liking himself, and in his anger, because he was not watching, he stepped on a thorn. It penetrated his foot, but he did not cry out—no Nuer would.

He stopped to take it out. His anger left him with the thorn, as if it had been punishment and punishment enough for now. Something else had gone too. His friendship with Cor was over, he knew.

He got up and walked beside the cattle.

The day gradually came to a close. There had been no rest and no food for the herdsmen, but they did not care. Their reward came with sight of the village. They had arrived. The snakes, the flies, the lions, the rifts and holes in the ground—all hazards had been met, and all had been overcome. They were home!

"I only want to sleep and rest!" An exhausted Jany threw himself down on the cool, clay floor of their house and closed his eyes. His father, who had come to greet him, laughed and let him lie. He was proud of his son.

Soon the women would come with the goats and the sheep. He lit the fire and set out the pots and gourds for his wife. He was ready for her. The corn had been planted and would soon show above the ground; the beans were already sprouting. The leaks in the roof had been repaired. He would kill another ox—one that he had captured—and they would manage until they had durra again.

Jany looked around for Pan, but Pan was not there. He was readying the cattle for the night. After their long journey the cows were tired and edgy in this place they did not know was home. As Pan milked them, he smoothed their backs. Then he built a fire in the center of the cattle house. When it was smoking he led the cattle into it. The smoke would keep them free of mosquitoes and they could rest.

In the gathering dusk the lowing of cattle mingled with calls of greeting and mothers singing to babies. The smoke of cooking fires rose into the evening air and made the village misty as people and animals sought their rest. While Pan stroked and petted the cows, someone watched him. It was Jany's mother. She murmured to herself:

"He is a Dinka—like my people."

73

Everyone rose early and worked late, but the time seemed to slip by as the days melted into each other. The boys carried off dirt from the ditches and, now that the rain had softened the ground, they took over the weeding of the corn that Jany's father had begun. They followed him up and down the rows dropping durra seed into the holes he dug to receive them. They carried water and they carried dirt and they carried ashes and kept the byre clean. It had become their job to watch the cattle, for they ate the new grass around the byre and in the nearby fields that separated their house from the others in the village. Milking and churning and gathering and sweeping—a merry-go-round that kept them all moving with hardly time to speak to one another.

This afternoon, hot and steamy and still wet from the morning rain, Jany sought the coolness of their house, and as he lay stretched on the clay floor, his mother brought him milk to drink and put some reeds under his head from the pile she was plaiting for the storage baskets they would soon need.

Jany, his eyes closed, could still see the yellow earth he had worked in for so long. Whether dry or muddied by rain, the ground seemed to be his only world now.

"You will rest when all is done, and we will watch the durra grow. This year is a good year—and not hard."

Jany started to protest, but smiled at her instead. Perhaps she was right.

"This year the rains are good to us—there will be more seed than ever before. What of the years—I remember them too well—when, after the work of the sowing and planting and weeding, there was nothing for us to harvest?"

As she worked on her basket, she went on talking, her voice lulling Jany. "You cannot remember—you were little when it happened—the year of the grasshopper. Five times we planted our crop that year. The first time when our seeds were in the ground they did not grow. No rain came to make them live and they turned to dust.

"Again we dug the hard earth, again we carried water and again we planted. The rains came—but this time the lightning came too, and struck the house. We had no roof and could not stop to build one.

"After the storms—oh, the crashing and the blowing of the storms!—the seed grew. The first leaves brought the grasshoppers. The sky turned black with them—they were everywhere—in our ears, under our feet, on the walls, in our bowls of food.

"Then they were nowhere. And there were no leaves, no grass . . . Again we put our seed into the ground and again the new plants grew. And again the grasshoppers came and again there was nothing for us.

"When we planted yet again and the plants grew anew and the weeds grew, we loved even the weeds, for they were green and there had been no green until then.

"We had a harvest that year too. We were fortunate —we had enough." She stopped, for Jany had fallen asleep. She bent down to kiss him, and said to the sleeping boy, "This is a good year for us."

When Jany awoke it was dark in the house, but outside there was a little light and people still worked. Jany's father would work until it was too dark to see.

Sighing, Jany dragged himself up and went to get the gourds. It must be milking time. As he headed for the byre he thought how he had chafed at this task. Women's work he had called it, but now that he was too weary to straighten his shoulders in pride, he thought what difference does it make. Women's work, men's work—hands must find the task nearest and do what had to be done.

* * * * *

Sometimes they worked with the rain on their backs, or knee-deep in mud. They hunted for what wood there was for their fires. Dung would not dry in the wetness of the rains. They fought off the mosquitoes which tormented them constantly—there seemed to be millions of them. They climbed on the bird platforms that had

been built and spent hours shooing off the flocking birds that seemed to spring from the earth. The bird platforms were really needed this year. To the weary boys—and to the men—there was too much to do.

Then one day Jany looked at their fields. The clouds scudded past overhead, casting shadows over the recently sown earth, and kept their burden of water for another day. There is water enough for growing plants, they seemed to be saying.

Wherever there was space for seed, there was seed. The corn was growing between the rows of durra that was beginning to show above the ground. Beans were waiting to be picked. The ditches they had dug were holding the water of yesterday's rains and were deep enough to carry off more water when it came.

There were no weeds. The byres were clean. It had all been done!

8

The Stranger

It did not rain every day during the rainy season. One bright morning when a breeze ruffled the ripening grain, made the cowbells tinkle, and cooled the faces of the old men sitting in the sun smoking their pipes, Jany's father called to him.

He said, "Some day you will own cattle. It may be a large herd and they will eat many grasses. I want you to know which are the best. Not all are good and some are to be watched for. There is grass that makes sheep grow large with swelling and die. You must learn to see it before the sheep do."

Jany's father gazed out over the land he felt was his and which he loved. He paused as if weighing the task of telling his son all he knew. It would take many walks in the grass. But it was time to begin. "Call Pan," he said, "and we will go."

Jany found Pan throwing stones, bits of hard mud and pieces of wood at the greedy birds from the bird platform. Children ran after the stones and brought them back, for there weren't many stones in Nuerland and they had to be saved and used again and again. He jumped down when he saw Jany and ran to him.

"You want me?" Pan asked eagerly.

"My father does," Jany replied, and saw the smile vanish. Jany wanted him to come too, but he couldn't say it.

When they joined Jany's father, they set off gaily. It was like a holiday—a rare golden day when there were no fields to tend and people were not too busy for each other.

The grass had grown so tall in the rains that last year's trails were lost, and Jany's father slashed at the tallest of it with his spear to clear a path for them.

Jany learned which grasses the cows liked best and which made them give the sweetest milk, which grasses could quench their thirst when they weren't near water and which would make them fat.

Jany's father sank down upon one knee and picked a spray of stems like a lady's fan, for them to see. "This is poon," he said. "You have eaten it many times." And he loosened the ripening grains of wild rice so they ran through his fingers.

The small bright flowers of wild jute shone in the grass like coins, and clusters of pink flowers rained magic on them as they brushed past the tall stems. Everywhere there was the smell of wild hibiscus.

They listened to the chattering monkeys in the branches over their heads when they walked under the acacias, and they heard the call of the go-away bird. They saw the huge nests of the weaver birds, large enough for Jany to fit into. Sometimes they sank into hidden pools or felt a nest with their feet. In this grass they loved there was always a mystery just a step ahead.

The grass was full of seed. It was indeed a good year for all the grain, wild as well as their durra. The durra birds, the seed-eaters, fluttered overhead when their nests were disturbed.

"I have never seen so many nests," Jany's father told them as he stopped in the grass again. "Look here—and here—and here." An uncertain feeling, almost a fear, began inside of him. Why were there so many this year? Where did they come from?

Jany found an ostrich nest and they took some eggs, not to eat, for this would not seem right to a Nuer, but to make bracelets out of the shells.

It was time to turn back. It had been a good day for all of them and Jany was happy. Impulsively he held out the eggs and showed them to Pan. "I will make a bracelet for you too." Pan's eyes gleamed and his lips parted, but he said nothing. Jany had already run away.

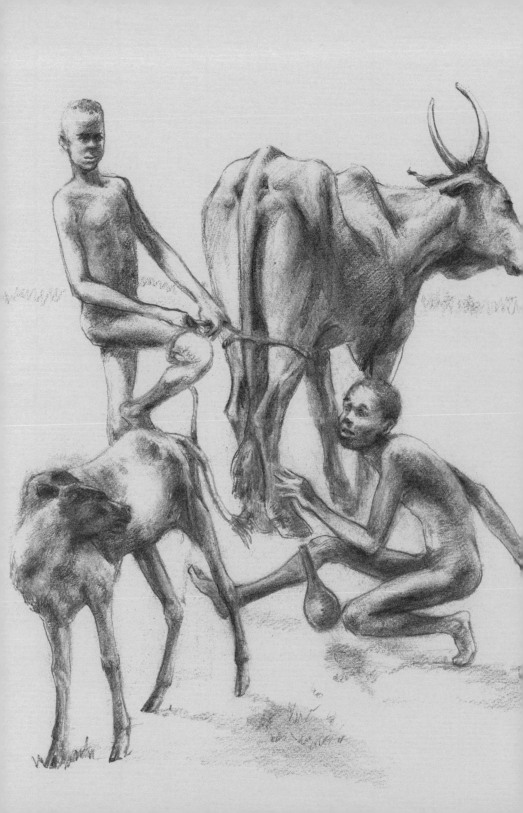

Jany went with Pan to help with the milking when they had returned to their village. A white calf with a black head nuzzled Jany when he tried to milk its mother. It had been interrupted from nursing and tried to push Jany away.

"Isn't he beautiful," Jany asked Pan. The calf sent him sprawling, but Jany still loved it. "I have named him 'Ku-Ee' for the eagle whose clan-name is ours," Jany told Pan.

It would not be long before this calf would be full-grown. It would be an ox to be proud of by the time of Jany's initiation rites. It would be his and he would take its name when he got his spear. He would make tassels out of the silk of new corn for it.

"Pan, which ox will give you its name? Do you know yet—have you picked one?" Jany asked eagerly. "The initiation may be after the rain of the next planting— that is not very far off!"

The nearness of it was almost breathtaking. Jany lost himself in dreams of his spear and his coming manhood and the wonderful things he would do when he was as tall as his father. He was not aware that Pan had given no answer to his question—nor joined him in his excitement about the forthcoming initiation.

It was not until his eyes were almost closing that night on the platform in the byre where he and Pan slept, that he remembered his question. He watched Ku-Ee through the smoke and imagined that the calf said good night to him even as he bid it a good night.

"Pan," he said, "you must have one you love among these. Tell me which it is. We will think of a name and I will help you write a song to it that we can sing together."

He heard no answer from Pan.

"Tell me," he persisted. Still no answer. Jany leaned over and touched Pan's shoulder. "Pan?" he whispered. Pan's face remained buried in his arms, and he did not turn his head even then, but he was saying something. Jany had to bend lower to hear it.

"I can have no ox nor can I take an ox-name. I cannot be initiated with you for I am . . . I am a stranger. I do not belong." Pan's voice was very low, but not too low for the anger and bitterness in it to be heard. "I am not your brother."

"Brother!" The word startled Jany. His thoughts went back over the weeks that had just gone by. The weeding, the planting, the new threshing floor that they had made out of clay gathered from the ditches they had themselves dug. Caring for the cows, the milking—they had shared their tasks, they had even shared their food. Jany had gone hungry at times so that Pan could eat also.

Now he was used to Pan being with him, even during those rare times when there was no work and when he just sat and listened to the rain or counted the flamingoes in the sky.

Above his head, curls of smoke gathered in the rounded dome of the byre as they tried to reach the smoke-hole at the top. Perhaps it was this that made his eyes water—this bitter smoke that formed pictures in the air and awoke memories that made him ashamed.

He listened to the hooves of the cattle as they stirred on the hard clay floor, and he heard again his own haughty tone when he had first spoken to Pan. He recalled the orders he had given as if to a slave, the scornful laughter when Pan was awkward.

Jany squirmed. He had not wanted to remember so much, but there was no way to stop the pictures from forming in his mind.

The brother he once had, died when he was just a young boy. Jany himself was still crawling among the legs of the lambs and little goats in the kraal when smallpox took this brother. Smallpox had taken many lives that year.

Jany knew nothing of this brother, for his people did not speak of the dead. To do so, they said, would make God think they were angry at him for taking a loved one. So the little grave had been beaten flat with rice stalks. Dust had been spread over it and nothing left to mark it. He remembered him when he was lonely. He was lonely no longer. He had a companion.

Why do I not say that I am glad Pan is here and that I would be lonely without him? Because he came as a captive and stayed as a servant. Because we laugh at Dinkas and he is one. Am I ashamed to like someone who is a Dinka? Jany asked himself, angry at last at his own doubts. "If he left, I would miss him. I do not want him to go," Jany thought. "Then he is my friend." His own logic was clear—certainly to him.

It had started to rain. The sunshine was only an interlude. The noise of the storm on the roof grew in intensity as if it had to make up for its absence that day. A great peal of thunder rocked the byre, and for a moment it was brilliant with lightning. Again the thunder roared. The frightened cattle began to bellow; the noise of the wind-driven rain grew louder.

Jany saw Pan sitting up, the frightened look that had been on his face when he had first come was there again. He was bewildered, for he had been startled out of his sleep by the fury of the storm and for the moment did not know where he was.

He caught sight of Jany. His face relaxed. A sleepy smile spread over his face, and he closed his eyes again.

Jany remembered how, when there was thunder in

the sky and howling winds raced over the plains, his fright had gone away if he touched his father's hand—or saw him close by. He knew then that Pan had not only forgiven him, but had come to love him.

He promised himself that he would be what Pan thought him. He vowed that he would never again let anyone hurt Pan or call him names. Jany, at peace with himself, at last closed his eyes and slept.

Pan fell back into his dream as if he had never left it.

9

Hungry Birds

The village seemed deserted. Nobody could be seen along the long stretch of road that connected the houses. The only sound was a baby's laughter from inside one of the houses and the low murmur of old women gossiping about their youth. It was reaping time, and everybody who could reach the stalks was in the fields.

The durra was not fully ripe yet but they did not want to wait any longer for it. It was the first crop—the one most eagerly awaited. Besides, they knew that if you pinched off an ear that is not fully ripe, no seed will fall from it to the ground and be wasted.

Jany's mother, her basket laden, called Gia to her and together they went back to the house. "We will get the floor ready for the threshing. There will be much durra for it before the end of this day," she said to the girl.

Gia nodded and together they got down on hands and knees and smoothed the floor. With careful hands they felt for grass and dust or stones and brushed them away so they would not mix with the durra when it was threshed.

When they spread it out to dry, Gia knew it would make them proud and glad of the long hours of work it had taken to grow it. When it was dry enough, it would be beaten with heavy sticks to loosen the grain. Then it would be left to dry again on the floor.

It would be winnowed. Jany's mother had made winnowing screens out of reeds and stalks. The durra would be thrown against the screens, the grain falling down, the chaff carried off on the wind.

All this had to be done before Gia could take it and grind it into flour. The boys had dug a hole and lined it with clay and it lay ready for the grain, like a sunken bowl waiting to be filled. It was hard, slow work, this grinding. Jany's mother would spend many hours pressing the huge club on the grain, leaning with all her weight as she brought the heavy club with its rounded end down on the grain—again and again and again.

Storage baskets were waiting on tall piles of stones gathered very carefully in this land where stones were scarce. They were high so that the rats would not nibble holes in them and let the grain spill to the floor before it could be used.

Even as the first crop was being reaped, even before any durra had been spilled over the threshing floor, the men talked of planting their second crop. Some had already begun. Each minute of growing time must be put to use if they were not to go hungry when the dry time came again. Where could these people seek help if not from themselves? If they starved who would know and who would bring food?

There was much to do, and the days ran swiftly into each other. The rains came often. "It is always raining," they said, and rubbed themselves with ashes to lessen the sting and torment of the flies—especially the seroot whose bite was so vicious it drew blood from the thick hide of the cattle. The mosquitoes were still with them too.

On bare feet they walked in mud to bring grass to the cattle who grew fat in their byres. The cattle were not let out to walk in mud lest it hurt their feet.

"There is time for everything," Jany's mother used to say as she worked, and watched the others to see that they were busy too. "There is time, if your hands are never still."

A day came even during the rainiest time of the year when the sun shone, and on this day Gia stood over the grain in the hole and ground it. Up and down, her club pounded the grain as she kept time with a song.

Gee's little sister watched her. It seemed that wherever Gia was, she was to be found as well. She liked to watch Gia and when Gee sent her with messages to Gia she ran happily to do his bidding.

As she stood and watched she knew that some day she would be doing just as Gia was doing. She knew that one day she too would be tall and beautiful and that someone would wait in the fields where the grass was tall enough to hide him and whistle for her to come as Gee did often now.

She knew that her brother was watching Gia, though he could not be seen himself. Jany's mother knew he couldn't be far. Gee could not come to the house, for this would not be seemly. It would not be right for him to speak to the man who would be his father-in-law. He would not sit with Jany's father or take food from him, for respect for him was too great. It grew with his love for Gia, and he loved her family as well. He had long since forgotten that Gia had not been born in this village to these people. To Gee she was not a stranger nor had he ever thought of her by any name than her own, her true name.

Jany's mother heard his low whistle now, though she still could not see him. His little sister heard it too. Yet Gia seemed not to have heard and worked even harder, lifting her club and bringing it down—up and down—up and down.

"That is enough," Jany's mother said kindly, and

Gia dropped the mallet and was gone like a flash toward the spot where the whistle had come from.

Jany's mother smiled to herself. Then with a sigh she turned back to her work. If it did not rain, the grain would be dry enough for threshing tomorrow.

She glanced at the clouds in the sky. They were fleecy and looked innocent. But there on the horizon was something else—not rain clouds, but blacker than thunderheads and far more fearsome. On the far horizon, she saw a black mass of countless birds, looking as if caught in a net of colored mist.

"Never have I seen so many," she said to herself, her hands pressing against her beating heart. Were there more than even her sharp eyes could see? "Every year we are troubled by birds when our seed is ripe. This year is no different," she told herself. But she grew calm not with her words, but because the cloud did not come nearer. It seemed instead to be disappearing over the horizon.

There was no moon that night. At reaping time everyone sought his rest early. Jany's mother stirred in her sleep, muttering, groaning, tossing restlessly. Gia woke and shook her gently to free her from whatever dreams disturbed her rest.

She opened her eyes and was immediately wide awake. "Come," she whispered and rose from her bed.

93

Gia followed her to the granaries. She picked up her earthen pots, filled them with seed from the baskets, and with Gia's help took them to the byre. Then they stole back to their beds and their rest.

As Jany's mother settled herself for sleep, she said to Gia, "I had a dream of clouds without rain that darkened the sky and drank up everything we had—but I feel better now." She patted Gia's cheek. "I will sleep."

The rains came again in the early morning, and when they ceased, the rising sun shone over the wet grass and drew colored sparks from it; the mists were gold and pink and violet, and a softly shimmering green nearest the horizon hung in the air, turning their land into a dreamlike place.

Gia stood in the doorway and looked at the new morning. She did not see at first the huge black cloud rising again on the horizon. But Jany's mother saw it, and her eyes grew great with wonder and dismay.

The dark cloud grew, spread out, came together again. It moved like an accordion. It rose, thinned out over the sky, came together into a dense blackness. And always, it grew and grew and grew. Another cloud rose in the north. It too spread, flattened, spread out again like smoke from a huge funnel claiming the freedom of the skies for itself. Another cloud. Another. There was no longer north or south, east or west. Birds were every-

where—a plague of birds. The durra-birds had come to feast on their fields.

These birds were known to them all. They had been a familiar and a friendly presence always underfoot, their chirping a part of the sounds of the village. Now these little harmless birds had become horrible. They shut out the sun. They turned the land into a whirring, flapping inferno of noise. They chattered and jostled and crowded and fought each other in their desperate greed. There were too many for any land to feed. There could not be enough seed in the world for so many birds.

A cracking sound! A branch laden with birds, one on top of another, had broken under their weight and crashed to the ground, killing the birds with it and almost killing people beneath it.

The noise startled the people, watching the waves of birds with terror, into frenzied action. Children started to cry, cattle bellowed as birds covered their backs and pecked at their hides for whatever stray seeds might be there, dogs barked in pain—and somewhere out in the grass a frightened hyena uttered a hideous laugh.

A voice could be made out above the din. Jany's father was shouting to them, trying to get them to listen. "To the roofs! To the roofs! The birds will break in the roofs! We must clear the roofs! Get the cattle into the byres! Quickly, quickly!"

Jany shooed animals through the rain of birds. Everybody was busy now, and some sort of order began to form. Children were hastily picked up and pushed through whatever doorway there was—the cattle hustled into the byres.

Jany's father climbed to the top of a byre, his spear in his hand, and started to swing it over his head in wide circles to chase the birds back in the air. His legs were spread apart to give some ballast on the rounded roof, and though he sometimes faltered, his spear never stopped moving.

The fields could not be saved, but if they could keep the birds from collapsing into the byres and the houses and keep them from stampeding the cattle, it might yet be called a victory.

Now there was someone on every roof. It looked like a dance, this rhythmic waving of spears and sticks and poles among the flocking birds.

Pan and Jany worked furiously, crowding what they could into the houses. Then they too took their positions on a roof—it did not matter that it was not theirs. Whatever was saved would benefit all. But they were sweeping back the sea. For every bird forced into the sky, fifty returned. Furious at being kept from their seed, they clawed each other and everything that got in their way.

Sometimes, through a break in the thick whirling masses of black feathers, Jany could see his father still swinging his spear. It seemed to Jany that he had never known a time that wasn't full of screeching, of flapping wings, of pecking beaks. Birds roosted on his head, on his shoulders, climbed on his back, their wings brushed against his face, struck his eyes, his ears. One tried to fly into his open mouth.

It was never going to end. He had been waving his stick forever . . . His eyes started to close, he slumped forward and would have fallen had it not been for Pan's arm that was suddenly around him.

It had become a struggle just to keep awake. Time passed slowly, no one had eaten, no one had rested. Woman huddled with the children in the byres below and tried to calm the crowded, frightened cattle. Everyone else fought the birds. They could not win—but how could they stop trying?

Jany's father still stood, legs spread wide apart, his spear brandished high. It seemed that any man must have wearied long before this, but there he stood.

Jany, tears of exhaustion rolling down his cheeks, took strength from his father's example and kept on, waving his stick, shouting at the birds and hating them with all his heart.

It would soon be dark. The birds smelled night in the air and their instinct, stronger than their greed, started to draw them back to their roosting places in the far-off grasslands.

"Just a little longer! A little longer and they will be gone! Just a little!" Jany's father shouted to the exhausted men around him. As if to hearten them with his own actions, he swung in a wide arc. Too wide! He teetered, swayed, lost his balance, fell from the roof.

Jany saw his father go down and he could only stand and watch. He heard a scream. It was his own.

10

All Is Lost

It was a warm, soft night. In the village everything was quiet. The birds had gone as suddenly and as unexpectedly as they had come. They would not come again. There was no seed left.

Now in the ravaged village, life was stirring again. Cows had been fed and milked. Children were being wooed to sleep by their exhausted mothers. The words of a song, sad and slow, drifted in the evening air, and the blessed dark brought peace to the weary. The ruined fields, the empty granaries were all around them. Tomorrow was another day. Now it was time to rest.

But there was no peace in Jany's house. His father lay on a goatskin, his arms rigid at his sides, his fists clenched, his eyes shut tight. He had made no outcry after his fall, not even when he had been carried into his house, his right leg twisted into an unnatural position. He could not move it.

Jany looked at him and knew that he had never seen

his father so grim, so tense, so unlike himself. Worse for him to see was his mother. She sat by her husband's side, rocking gently back and forth, tears rolling down her cheeks into her upturned hands lying limply in her lap.

She had not cried when she had held her firstborn in her arms and had felt him stiffen and grow cold with death. No tears had rolled down her face when she had stood with her husband and they had counted their dead cattle the year the jungle let the sickness into their land.

Sickness from the jungle had come again and taken her brothers one terrible year. Still she had helped dig their graves and had not cried.

She had seen her father carried out of the river, out of his boat stuck fast in the papyrus after a crocodile had reached him. She had not been allowed near him. She could still remember her mother's voice, "Do not cry. Tears are your enemies. You blame God with tears so you must not cry. God does not want you to cry."

She remembered the words, but now tears ran down her face, unchecked by pride or fear. Everything was ruined—all was lost—and her husband lay helpless in his pain. She could do nothing.

There were friends who were helping. Rol, his father's friend, had run far during the night to find a man known everywhere for his power to heal. Rol found him in the midst of ruin and a desolate people, for that village had been overrun as well. The man listened to Rol, and started off with him into the night without a word.

The dawn had not yet broken when he entered the house with Rol behind him. His dark, probing eyes looked around him and fell on the one in pain. He knelt at his side and gently ran his fingers up and down the oddly bent, swollen leg. He asked for stalks and reeds to be brought to him and when they were in his

hands, he deftly wove them into a basket the size of the injured leg. It was very strong, though light and flexible.

Then he addressed the room. "He must be held very still so that I can straighten the leg where it is broken."

Jany held his father's hands, Rol leaned across his chest. There was no sound as the doctor worked, just a great intake of breath like a silent scream when the bone was snapped back into place. Quickly then, the leg was wrapped in the basket which served as splint and cast. It would keep the leg still and let it heal.

It was beginning to be light. The sounds of a waking village drifted into their house. Jany's mother, hearing the low murmur of voices outside, wiped her eyes and went to see who had come.

Before their house stood the head man of their village. He was in his leopard skin, for he had come on an important mission. He was going to sacrifice a bull to ensure the recovery of Jany's father. Jany's mother, her voice toneless, her eyes downcast, told him to select any animal he wished.

She turned away and with a heavy sigh returned to her husband's side. Gia tried to comfort her and pressed her hands. "Do not forget," she whispered, "we have seed to plant. I have seen it in the earthen pots inside the byre and there is enough. The birds did not get it all."

It was true. Jany's mother had forgotten what they had done. There was seed, and if there was seed there was hope. She looked gratefully into Gia's eyes and touched her face.

Jany saw the change in his mother. He breathed again, his tense body relaxed, his eyes closed for a moment in grateful relief. For a moment tears were close to falling. He went outside.

The morning had come and its light revealed a scene that made him forget his tears. He could only stare in sudden shock. It had started to drizzle, and under the gray sky the bedraggled land was more desolate than anything he had ever seen before. The crazily scattered rubble, the broken branches, a house with caved-in roof—for not every house had been saved—the bird platforms destroyed by the birds. The ditches were full of dead rats and mice that had been crushed to death by the weight of birds. Feathers lay on everything—and hundreds of dead birds covered the ground. Jany wanted to run to his mother and bury his head in her lap. He stood there and looked at the awful scene, shaken, uncertain which way to turn.

A chilly wind blew dead grass and ruined stalks against his legs. He picked up a stray milking gourd that lay at his feet. It was too much to bear! In sudden anger he hurled it at the side of the byre and ran blindly ahead, the stubble cutting his feet and making him cry.

"Jany!" He stopped. It was Pan's voice. "Here, Jany."

He turned around and saw Pan. Pan was on his knees in the ruined field, his hoe beside him, sweeping together dead birds, dead stalks, tattered roots into a pile of rubble. He was clearing the fields so that they could plant again.

As Jany watched, he realized that this was no time for tears. Standing there in the rain under leaden skies, his courage returned, and as Pan smiled at him he was able to hold up an arm in greeting. After all, he thought, the cows had all been saved—there might be bush yams left in the grass to find. Their houses were still there. It was not too bad.

The cows! Jany realized they had not been tended. He picked up the gourd he had thrown and started for them; already forgotten was the despair of a few moments ago.

Pan turned back to his work.

* * * * *

Once again the fields were cleared and planted and the seeds were given life by the earth that does not know failure and does not stop giving. There would be durra again.

When the new grain was at last on the stalks, a day soon followed when it had to be ground into flour, and once again Gia lifted her heavy club—up and down, up and down. The rainy season was almost over and the time of feasting had begun. There was much to be grateful for, and the feasts would be happy.

Jany's mother came for the flour, and as she stooped down for it, she said to Gia, "We will need more—much more." She looked up at Gia and smiled. "There must be beer for the wedding, you know."

Shyness and joy lit up Gia's face, "I thought—Gee could not speak until—surely, he would not speak of a wedding until the leg has been healed. Has he spoken?"

Jany's mother took Gia's hand and said, smiling to her, "Come and I will show you something," as she pulled her to the door of the house.

Gia looked inside, and though it was dark she saw what Jany's mother wanted her to see. The tall man standing there, leaning on both Pan and Jany, was Jany's father. Jany's mother whispered to her, "He stood up when Gee came!"

Gia could not speak. She did not know how it had come about that all she had desired was now hers— people who loved her and whom she loved as her family and a future that held so much happiness. She would never know or understand, but she knew the gratitude in her heart.

Jany's mother walked into the house. "No more steps!" she spoke with authority. While her husband had lain helpless she had taken charge, and all had learned to obey her. Her husband minded her words and did as she told him. He did her weaving and he churned butter and he made pots and he would say, "Yes, yes," when she brought him new things to do with his hands. He said "Yes, yes," when she told him to eat, to rest, to sleep. And always he would smile. He smiled most when her demands grew loudest. Jany did not understand, but it seemed to him that his father enjoyed it all.

"Back to work, all of you," Jany's mother now addressed them. "Have you never seen a man stand up before?" She shooed them out as if they were gawking calves. "He can take a step—yes—but can he milk, can he weed the fields? Why are you standing about?"

Pan and Jany obeyed though they dragged their hoes after them as if they were as heavy as full water gourds. Outside the sun was shining, and it seemed to beckon to other things than weeds. They started for the fields—they did not want to work. They were, after all, young, and though they had been as serious and perhaps worked even harder than grown men, they were not yet grown men.

They dropped their hoes with one accord. Jany fashioned a hoop out of stalks and sent it sailing into the air and they ran after it aiming stones and bits of mud at it.

"Here, catch this," Pan called as he swung at a mud ball Jany threw at him. His hoe made a good bat, and his aim grew better. Jany rubbed his head where one of his own balls had landed.

At last Jany stopped, streaming with sweat and panting, and they went to get milk. They found Ku-Ee pulling at his mother's teats and, pushing him aside, they held a gourd under the willing cow and drank the sweet milk she gave them. Jany stroked Ku-Ee and let him lick his fingers still wet with milk.

"You are like the black raven lost in a white cloud bank," he said to his calf. "You are white cream that spills over the black ground when the milking is best. You are beautiful—you are like dark water when it is covered with white lilies." He was enamored of the little calf, and more compliments formed on his lips, but suddenly he remembered Pan, standing behind him.

Pan had no ox. The joy Jany felt shriveled within him. As they left the kraal, Jany stroked the side of a red-brown cow.

"Red is for happiness," he said mechanically, but he was not happy.

Pan, not aware of Jany's changed mood, fashioned new mud balls and threw them, one at a time, his arm making a wide arc. Then he ran to catch each one before it fell to the ground. He was suddenly aware that something, or someone, was in his path, but it was too late to stop. He was going too fast and he ran headlong into Jany's father.

Horrified, Pan reached out to steady him, realizing as he did that his impact had knocked the stick Jany's father leaned on out from under his arm. Jany ran to pick it up.

The boys were afraid to look at his face as they held

him up. Jany hunched his shoulders and waited for the storm of anger to break over his head.

But the sound that came to Jany's ears was not the sound of anger. He could not believe his ears. It was laughter.

"So," his father said, "I have caught you out. Both of you—just as bad as Rim the hyena, who plays tricks and never works!"

Pan was looking at him, the old frightened strained look on his face once more. He had been wrong, and though he heard the laughter and the bantering words, he felt he had no right to them.

Jany's father still held his arm around Pan. He pushed Pan away a little and looking down at him, he said very seriously, "Pan, you are a good boy. You gave us courage when we needed it most."

Jany was watching them intently. Jany's father turned to him, "Jany, I came here to ask you to look for wood so we could make fiddles. We will make music when we celebrate our good fortune. We have many things to celebrate, have we not, son?"

Jany nodded. Jany's father still held Pan by the shoulders and Pan looked at him bewildered, not knowing what to make of this. Jany's father was still speaking.

"Pan, I want to make you my son. In this time of feasting we will hold an adoption ceremony and this will

give us more joy than all the other feasts together. I know Jany wishes this too."

Pan threw his arms around Jany's father and buried his head against his chest. Then he turned and ran into the grass. He had to be alone with his happiness for a little while. He ran heedlessly, tripping, falling, getting up, only to fall down again and to roll over and over in the warm grass as if the earth embraced him.

Jany watched, but did not follow him. Nor did he return to the house with his father. He wanted to think about what had happened. He walked away from the fields and in a little clearing, he lay down and watched, through half-closed eyes, the patterns of the grass against the sky as they shifted and moved in the breeze. He heard the buzzing of bees gathering honey from the hibiscus and the humming of hundreds of insects singing in the grass.

His eyes closed. As he lay there the shadows of clouds sailed past overhead and blotted out the sun. A shadow fell across him, but it did not sail on as the others had, for it was not cast by a cloud. Jany knew who stood there before he opened his eyes to see. He had a brother!

He stood up. Without a word between them the two boys turned and walked home together.

11

We Are All the Same

Jany had made his first fiddle. His mother held it up against the sky and hastily put it down again. It had looked even more uneven that way than it had on the ground.

"It will make beautiful music," she said. There was nobody who would say she was wrong. Who would dare?

Gee's family was coming for the wedding talk on the next day. Before there could be a wedding, the families had to meet and they had to settle that most important of all questions, the bride-price. Oxen and cows had to be offered and accepted before Gee's intentions could be taken seriously.

It seemed to Gia that nothing was ready for Gee's family. Her ears had to be pierced in five places so that they could carry the five little white stones that would mark her as a married woman. Where was the grass for her new skirt? Beads lay about still unstrung. Would there be enough beer? And meat—no animal had been slaughtered yet for the guests.

Jany's mother had given Gia all her beads and had made her a fan of ostrich feathers. Bracelets of ostrich eggshells, giraffe hair, and silver from the Arab traders were ready for her. Gia's hair had been bleached and was now red-gold in color and tomorrow would be decorated.

Gia wanted these new people to like her. As she looked at her growing fortune of ornaments, a doubt inside of her could not be silenced. Would these make any difference, after all?

The next morning came too soon for her. Laden with beads—they had been strung together in time!—she stood at attention as Gee's family arrived. She looked so stiff and strange that Pan hardly recognized his sister. He did not know that these strangers who were arriving could, with one sign of affection, change this stiff girl into the Gia he knew.

Gee's relatives sat and took the beer offered them. The goat killed last night was roasting in a pit of ashes and its aroma filled the air. The wedding talk began amid good smells and generosity.

Jany's attention wandered. It was hot, he was sleepy. There had been no sleep for any of them amid so many preparations. He did not understand the talk and idly

wondered why arranging a wedding that everyone
wanted should take so long and need so many words.

He realized that all was not going well. His father,
until now genial, had begun to frown. He stood up and,
leaning on his stick, drew himself up to his full height.
In spite of his leg and the support it needed he was very

dignified as he confronted his guests. Someone had said, "ja-ang," a term of no respect, and Jany's father was very angry.

"You are not offering enough for a girl like Gia. She understands well how to make a husband happy and she never tires of work. But what is much worse, you have called her 'Dinka,' even 'ja-ang.' I want you to know that she is one of us—for love has made her so."

His voice vibrated with the strain of controlling his anger. He pointed his finger at a man on the ground, Tar, whom he knew well.

"Do I hear you, Tar? Do you say the word 'ja-ang' and are you not the son of a Dinka? Do you forget that your father came from Dinkaland and was adopted into your family?"

Tar was uncomfortable. "It was long ago," he muttered.

Jany's father pointed at still another, "And you—was not your mother brought to us, just as Gia was? What of your father—and yours?" he continued, his finger pointing at each in turn.

Jany was listening in amazement. His father had not finished. But his anger was spent and he went on in softer tones, as his arm dropped to his side.

"What of these of whom I have spoken? Are they not good people? Was your mother, she who came from far away, was she not good to you? Or your brother born a Dinka, or your father. Did they not love you?"

He looked at his wife who had come and was standing next to him. "And did you not love them, even as I have loved this woman who is my wife and who was born of a Dinka woman?"

Jany was stunned. His mother—a Dinka?

If all this was true, if their blood had mingled so freely, why had he been taught to hate the Dinka?

As he listened to his father's words, questions crowded in upon him and he did not know where to turn for answers. What should he think about the people against whom so much had been said? More important to Jany was the question, what should he think of those who had said it?

Jany sought some place where he could be alone, and finally, sitting in the shade of a palm tree, he tried to understand. Things had seemed clear to him—now nothing was clear.

He had always wanted his spear, but now he knew that when he got it he would be expected to use it against people he could not hate. The Dinka in the villages across the Sobat and up the White Nile were strangers— they were no longer enemies.

He had hated them—or so he thought. He had hated without passion but simply because he had been expected to in obedience to some unwritten law that he had never questioned. Could he raise his spear in obedience too? And if he did not, was he a coward?

The thought that overrode all the others was his fear that his father would scorn him for his doubts. His father, so brave, so fearless, as tall as his spear. Jany had wanted to be like him. Now he did not know.

When Pan came looking for him, as at last he did, Jany still had no answers.

"It will be dark soon. Let us go back," Pan said and started to pull Jany to his feet.

"Pan, tomorrow Rol will kill a bull and there will be a feast for your adoption—and you will be a Nuer," Jany said. "When you get your spear, what will you do?"

"I do not know," Pan answered slowly. "But I want to tell you that when your father captured me, he raised no spear. I came with him and I came willingly because I had no place to stay. Your father raised his spear to kill a lion in the bush. He killed no other thing.

"Jany," Pan continued, "tomorrow I will become your brother and your father's son. I have wanted this. Now that I know you do not hate my people, I want this even more."

Jany could barely make out Pan's features in the dim twilight that had settled on the land, but he knew the look that would be on his face—a look at once fearful and proud—a look that asked for understanding but wanted it freely given.

He knew that Pan hated to kill any living thing. Jany remembered the soft brown eyes of the giraffe that had bent its head to drink in the river beside him on a day that seemed so long ago. He did not want to kill either.

"You are brave," Jany told Pan. "You are braver than I am, for you never hated—anyone here," Jany's hesitation was but momentary.

It had started to rain. The soft warm mist wet their bodies but still they walked slowly. The village looked very peaceful. The wet horns of the cattle glistened in the firelight. The gentle rain made a rainbow around the glow of fire as the firelight flickered and wavered.

It was hard to believe that raiding and killing were part of the life here. Jany knew that they could no longer be part of his life. There was Pan to help him know he was no coward. Who else would know?

* * * * *

Smoke rose on all sides and dimmed the horizon, much as the rain clouds had done in days gone by. The rains were over. It was time for the burning of the bush. The old grass was being cleared off the land the only way the Nuer knew. Another rainy season would bring fresh green again.

Across the smoking grasslands toward a village almost on the edge of the White Nile, Jany and Pan made their way. They had fallen behind the others, some of whom had already disappeared in the heavy mist that hung over everything.

They were going to get their spears. Their foreheads would be cut—three scars made across their brows would forever speak of their new manhood.

Jany felt no eagerness though he had dreamed of this day through most of the years that had passed for him. Where was he to find the enemies that should come with the honors that lay in wait for him?

Pan lifted his arm and pointed straight ahead. "It was from over there across the river that I came." The river was as wide as a lake after the rains. As Jany looked where Pan was pointing, he made out a steamer heading downriver.

"I saw many steamers when I lived here. They come often now."

"Where do they come from?" Jany too had seen steamers on the river, but not often, and it had not been part of his world and he had never asked what they meant.

"They come from Khartoum. They carry people back —sometimes to work in the fields. Sometimes to go to the schools."

Jany did not understand. "Schools?" he asked.

"I have not seen them, but I have heard many things told about them. They teach of other ways and other people." There was a new note in Pan's voice as he went on, "They teach of new ways to heal sickness, so that those who are sick do not have to go alone into the grass to die."

These boys, coming closer to an ancient tribal rite with each step, stopped to watch the steamboat disappear into the smoke that hung over the river.

Where was it going? Where was the world it could take them to? Jany's mind was forming a new idea—one that was too large to live on the grassland.

"Pan, some day we will see where the river goes."

They turned back to their destination, too busy with new thoughts to speak to each other.

The world was still far away, but the first step had been taken. When one wonders about something, one is halfway there.

About the Author

Leona Bond has brought to bear both her scientific and artistic disciplines upon this, her first book.

After receiving her B.A. at New York University, she did graduate work at the University of Zurich in Switzerland before beginning work on her doctorate in anthropology at Columbia University. Along with her studies in anthropology, she developed her skills as an artist by attending art school in Paris and the Art Students League in New York. Later, she became an illustrator with the Smithsonian Institution in Washington, D.C., and then a portrait painter.

Mrs. Bond's interest in the Nuers has been heightened by her association with authorities on African life. Her husband, an ornithologist, is the author of a number of works on the birds of Africa.

In her fieldwork with the Chinese and with the Indians on the Northwest coast, and in her contacts with other groups of people, Mrs. Bond became more and more impressed with how alike people are in spite of cultural differences, which are, she says, "after all, learned responses."

Mr. and Mrs. Bond and their daughter, Alissa, live in Alexandria, Virginia.